Suryanamskar
Program Your Body for wellness

Dr. Nitin Unkule

PUBLICATIONS

Suryanamaskar -
Program your body for wellness

First Edition: August 2015

Cover Design: Sandeep Deshpande

Design & Layout: Aman Torvi

Publisher: Sakal Publications
595, Budhwar Peth, Pune 411 002. (INDIA)

ISBN: 978-93-84316-47-1

For more information, contact:
020-24405678/88888 49050
sakalprakashan@esakal.com

Visit our website www.sakalpublications.com

Disclaimer: The views expressed in this book are those of the Authors and do not necessarily reflect the views of the Publishers.

I would like to dedicate this book to all my beloved Masters and Gurus who have been the inspiration of my life and who are 'the' authorities on all traditions and holders of all lineages. They are the revealers of the 'treasures' concealed by concrete faith and are an inexhaustible treasure-house of wisdom and compassion and inspired champions of Hinduism and the most vigorous missionaries in Bharat having variety of different weapons in their resourceful armory; as the sole guardian-angles of the Rishi-Culture.

Finally, I dedicate this book to all unseen and mighty powers and their mighty governors.

May this book help all who read it and spur them on their journey to wellness,and through wellness to enlightenment!

Foreword

Suryanamaskar: A boon for those who wish to maintain health.

Everyone wishes to maintain good health. A balanced diet, personal and environmental cleanliness, regular and adequate exercise and a peaceful, energetic mind enable an individual to achieve this aim.

Suryanamaskar is an excellent way to keep the muscles and joints of our bodies fit. Practically all parts of our body are put to action and exercised. *Suryanamaskar* helps to ventilate our lungs and maintain proper curvature and functions of the vertebral column. Digestion improves and constipation is corrected, sleep is sound.

The practice of *Suryanamaskar* does not require a special room or open ground. No special equipment or uniform needs to be purchased. Unlike outdoor activities, the state of the atmosphere and environment does not influence one's practice. There is no need to gather partners, though collective activity encourages social cohesiveness.

Reciting a prayer at the beginning of each *namaskar* encourages the building of faith. If music is concurrently played it helps to relieve fatigue. You have the option of doing *Suryanamaskar* for as much time as you wish to.

There is no doubt that *Suryanamaskar* is a great boon for the health of the body and mind.

Dr. H. V. Sardesai

CONTENTS

Preface

This book deals with one's most valuable asset, namely, health, without which success in any form brings no real joy and satisfaction in life.

Ancient Indian wisdom says that maintaining a work-life balance helps us to stay healthy, light in the body, bright in the head, and calm in the heart. According to the manuals of Vedanta and the ancient science of yoga, the human body is the most complex and unpredictable entity in nature. It needs certain adjustments and tuning up to function efficiently. The ancient sages and seers, *munis and acharyas* of India wrote down the precepts of living and dying in scriptural textbooks. Unfortunately, we no longer practice the age-old art of living and dying, and seem to have forgotten the fact that it is possible to die in good health.

The need of the hour is not only to achieve medical excellence and cure the sick and hapless, but also and perhaps more importantly, to prevent people from becoming sick in the first place. Some sections of society have been instilling fear into the minds of gullible people about diseases, disorders and ailments to get them into the net of drugs, insurance, and medical instruments. We must tell people the truth and let them live happily, devoid of fear. Everyone should know that there are valid alternatives to drugs, radiation and surgery.

Of course, none of us is going to live forever, but we do not have to suffer premature death, disability and the staggering expenses that follow a number of diseases of modern civilization. I have met a number of patients all over the world who would rather live with their disease after diagnosis than watch their helpless relatives be taken for a costly ride. We should all be surrounded by spiritual care and not medical care at the end of life. And if we wish to die, well then, we should know how to live well.

The concept of health, like that of life, cannot be defined precisely, but the two are closely associated. What is meant by health depends on one's view of the living organism and its relation to its external and internal environments. The main confusion of the medical approach is related to the disease-process and disease-origin, and the damage done by the disease process. It should be recognized that the most fundamental question in medicine is why disease occurs in the body, rather than how it operates or manifests after it has occurred; conceptually the origins of disease should take precedence over the nature of the disease process, illness and health.

The frustrating truth, as far as medical science is concerned is that the living body is the best pharmacy God has ever devised under the Sun. It produces all vital vitamins, chemicals, acids and juices, hormones, diuretics, tranquilizers, painkillers, sleeping pills, Vitamin D through the rays of the Sun, antibiotics and indeed everything manufactured by the drug companies; and it makes them much superior so far as strength, quality and quantity is concerned. Your body does not manufacture spurious drugs, it does not violate the laws, and the dosage is always right and given on time, with no side effects. Moreover, it doesn't require a doctor's prescription!

Lifestyle modification which affects the mind and body in a holistic fashion is the most valid solution to illness, while also ensuring wellness. This has been imparted for centuries through the spiritual and yogic way of life through which the *rishis* preserved the youthfulness of their bodies far into old age. I have lived a life without drugs, radiation and surgery, and one reason for this is the regular practice of the old and time-tested way of exercise called Sun-Salutation or *Suryanamaskar*. Not only does it keep our inner pharmacy healthy, it also saves one from external supplement drugs, which can ruin the kidneys in the long run.

Although it may be true that 'there is nothing new under the Sun', it frequently happens that we go through life without having seen all that the Sun shines upon. The exercise therapies of ancient India are based on a profound respect for self-healing; on the belief that the patient is a responsible individual who can himself initiate the process of getting well. When you start to assert control over your body and mind by regularly following the exercise regime of *Suryanamaskar*, the effect is holistic. Though *Suryanamaskar* and yogic sciences are as old and traditional as civilization, they have become popular in modern society as a means to achieve vigor and vitality. By persistent and sustained practice, anybody can achieve optimum health and reach the goal of perfect fitness. I am sure an exercise regime like *Suryanamaskar* will contribute to gaining health in a short span of time.

As a globe trotter promoting yoga and Vedanta in many countries, I am convinced that the best way for the world to solve its big problems is for people to take the lead in solving health issues in a holistic way. I dared to write this book only after practicing *Suryanamaskar* for forty years. You don't have to wait that long to begin practicing *Suryanamaskar* - it has been said that one great advantage of any exercise is that one is never too young or too old to begin! This ancient Indian form of exercise is simple and eco-friendly - it doesn't require a modern gym, gadgets or instruments, expensive clothes, or plastic or rubber mats.

The exercise routine outlined in this book is original in conception, simple in application, positive in results, and founded on the movements of the prehistoric era. I am confident that you will find a great deal of illuminating information in this book. But information is only one aspect of health and healing. My greater hope is that you will also find inspiration to optimize your health and to look with wonder at the Universe that is around you and within you, and to realize that you are central to its creation, perhaps more than you ever dreamed or thought.

Dr. Nitin Unkule

Acknowledgements

The concepts and ideas presented in this book took over 10 years to mature. I often felt that it was being written through me, rather than by me. More than with any other book, I believe this one could not have been written without the inspiration and support of the many remarkable teachers, patients and students that I have met all over the world. Some of these are mentioned in the book, and many more are not - I acknowledge them all.

I am especially indebted to:
Sri Uday Pendse
Dr. Mukund Bhole
H. H. Swami Satswaroopananda Saraswati
Poona Hospital & Research Center
Dr. H. V. Sardesai
Dr. Fritjof Capra
All my heart patients of Poona Hospital
All my students of Kaivalya Yoga Institute
Dr. Dean Ornish
H. H. Swami Purshottamananda Tirtha
Dr. P. V. Vartak
Dr. Gene Kieffer
Sri S. M. Jawadekar
Sri Gopi Krishna
Galaxy Cancer Research Center
Sri Vasant J. Unkule
Dr. Jagdish Hiremath

Introduction

I would briefly like to tell you how I became a yoga teacher and how this book came into existence. I was a very shy boy in my school and college days, unable to speak in public, and with low self-esteem and confidence. My own existence was hateful to me. My parents were illiterate and were unable to guide me and I had no Godfather. I had an intense fear of the future and this anxiety resulted in a psychosomatic effect, causing me to suffer from frequent acute acidity bouts.

Medication was my shelter, but though I took ayurvedic, homeopathic and allopathic medicines, nothing worked. I continued to suffer and was mentally miserable; this made my personality unpredictable and uncontrolled. I often thought of myself as inefficient and unable to react to external challenges. It was like being lost in an overgrown jungle. I became victim to every passing circumstance and vacillated aimlessly with no motivation to live.

The Transformation
One summer afternoon, I noticed a signboard near my house advertising yoga classes. With no options left to treat my chronic acidity problems, I signed up for the daily classes. It was as if that one signboard had brought sudden bliss to my sad mind.

Yoga was like the final ray of hope. The care and love given to me by my yoga Guru changed my life. Like the mulberry leaves which with time and patience turn into silk, I credit yoga and Vedanta for altering my mind.

Though I joined yoga classes and started practicing *Suryanamaskar,* the frailty and sickliness remained with me for several days. I interacted with my revered teacher and Guru, Sri Uday Pendse, who advised a change in my dietary habits to elevate the spirit and the mind. This was to be the most major turning point in my life. It was as if my destiny had come to meet me and I had the opportunity to embrace it. These pivotal moments became the starting point to shaping my destiny.

Even the first few lessons of *yogasanas* (yoga-postures) brought gifts for me. It was a feeling of lightness, calm and joy. Deep silence started spreading into my body, and I was amazed that such an experience could be felt even by beginners. The initial lessons itself showed me the potential of life. It was indeed transformative, as if someone opened a golden gate for me.

My Guru's methods comprehensively judged my personality and help transform my life's discordant notes into music by adjusting, regulating and controlling the inner subjective personalities that I had. Yogic science brought about a total redemption for me from my sufferings. The techniques in *Suryanamaskar* taught by my teacher are for self improvement and are directed towards the disciplining and strengthening of one's psychological and the intellectual entities. They helped remove the superstitious stupidities I gathered during my college days and improved my impoverished mental stamina and twisted intellectual faculties.

My body became my first instrument to know and understand *Suryanamaskar* and yoga. The slow process of change and refinement started from then and continues in my practice till date.

THE HIDDEN PHYSIOLOGY

In the deeper issues that are beyond space and time, we may all be members of one family, called the complex body. Ancient discoveries relating to the origin of human thoughts have implications for the health of the body. For instance, the real risk factors in heart attacks and cancer, according to research findings in the US, were not just cholesterol or sugar or other physiological elements, but deeper issues like old resentments in the mind, dissatisfaction with a job, divorce, a restless mind, etc. Human biology has its own original intelligence, which once triggered, leads to health.

Technological advances have made our lives so much more comfortable than before. However, health is the greatest casualty of this modern lifestyle. We have to deal with irregular working hours, irregular food timings, unhealthy eating habits, stress, tension and pollution, all of which take a toll on our health.

Our saints, sages and learned forefathers always stressed on the combination of a healthy body and healthy mind. Man's mind is spread in every cell of his body and it has been discovered that our thoughts have a great impact and implication on our health. When something goes wrong in the mind-body-intellect equipment or set up, lifestyle changes or modifications are needed to assist the human physiology to set things right. Small modifications in our lifestyle, in our day to day living and eating habits can and will go a long way to reverse the damage we inflict on our bodies.

We need to focus on promotive and preventive health care rather than curative health care! Ancient Indian traditions such as ayurveda and yoga are based on profound respect for self-healing and can help us stay healthy.

Yoga is a 5,000-year old practice. According to Patanjali (circa 500 BC), the codifier of the Yoga system, the practice of Yoga destroys the impurities of the body and mind, after which maturity in intelligence and wisdom radiate from the core of one's being to function in unison with the body, senses, mind, intelligence and consciousness. *Suryanamaskar*, for example, is a very efficacious way of combating the ills of a modern lifestyle.

SURYANAMASKAR: THE UNSEEN COMPANION FOR GOOD HEALTH

The ancient Indian tradition of Salutations to the Sun God, or *Suryanamaskar*, practiced and propagated by our *rishis* and sages is a miracle exercise. Regular practice of *Suryanamaskar* can do wonders for the body and mind. A complete exercise, *Suryanamaskar* works on the entire skeleton, trunk and torso.

The Musculoskeletal System-Marvel of Engineering

Let us look at this wonderful creation of God, the human body. The human body or the musculoskeletal system is really a marvel of engineering. Most of the Yogic practices and *Suryanamaskar* require fine and smooth control over the use of muscles, ligaments, tendons and joints. The well controlled use of a specific group of muscles during specific stages of *Suryanamaskar* brings about a particular movement; and the maintenance or holding of that particular stage with minimum amount of muscle tone, are the two important factors in the performance-cycle of *Suryanamaskar*. Because of this, all the three features of muscular activity, i.e., strength, skill and stamina are influenced by the practice of this exercise. Moreover, the gradual and sustained increase in the range and number of movements through various joints increases the flexibility of the body.

Extensive studies at our Yoga Institute have shown this to be true in almost all interventions in asymptomatic people suffering from orthopedic ailments. In a holistic dynamic system like the human body there are so many in-built mechanisms to self-correct the risk factors that most, if not all such persons, do not suffer at the end. Only in the unlikely event of the body's correcting system failing does the individual suffer from symptoms of any disease.

Is any single exercise best for all the decades of life? Most authorities will say it is *Suryanamaskar*. It's the simplest way I know for building good posture and a flat tummy, and moreover, it helps to stand tall all the time.

Even Six Seconds Will Help

Begin gently. But keep at it. Work up to it gradually. Experts say *Suryanamaskar* makes a person move enough to push his blood into every nook and cranny of the body. By doing a 'daily dozen' *Suryanamaskars* every morning, we can get all the exercise we need and keep ourselves in top condition.

In a German laboratory of physiology at George William College, where I gave a demonstration, it was discovered that a very small amount of the right exercise will start a muscle growing. If you contract any one of your muscles to about two thirds of its maximum power and hold that for six seconds once a day, the muscle will grow as fast as it can grow. In *Suryanamaskar,* we hold any one position or step for a few seconds. The practice of *Suryanamaskar* emphasizes body movement and regularity. Every muscle and joint that has the power to wiggle must be made to wiggle more.

20 to 30 years: Doing several repetitions of *Suryanamaskars* will dissipate surplus energy and ease tensions.

31 to 40 years: *Suryanamaskar* is widely recommended because it has two prime benefits: it sends the blood circulating throughout the entire system; and it helps to take the mind off daily work and family related tensions.

41 to 50 years: During these years, people tend to become lazy and slothful. A brief exercise period is recommended every day.

51 to 65 years: Before exercise or *Suryanamaskar*, bend over until the tips of your fingers touch the floor. Do it 50 times. Do the liver or stomach squeezer, twisting around back and forth, 50 times.

Over 65: Do a few deep breathing, *Pranayam* techniques for half an hour every day. Walking is also recommended.

In these modern times, all of us resort to time-and labor-saving machines for our daily activities, thus reducing our physical exertion to a minimum. As a result, our muscle development suffers, affecting our general health. Lack of sufficient muscular action results in softness, flabbiness, rigidity, and actual shortening of the muscles. This can lead to some of the most painful and crippling of human ailments, weaknesses and disorders.

When we are worried or alarmed, we tense our muscles, and the tension persists for a while, tightening and shortening the muscles. An exercise like *Suryanamaskar* can lengthen the muscles and help us loosen up.

Lower back pain or lumbago is one of the commonest of human ills. Many people experience weakness and/or stiffness of muscles due to a lack of activity or exercise. Where there is a muscle, there is need for movement. 'Movement is life and life is movement' is the modern orthopedic principle.

Anyone, anywhere can do *Suryanamaskar.*

Suryanamaskar energizes the entire neuro-glandular and neuro-muscular system of the body. Its regular practice ensures a balanced supply of oxygenated blood and perfect harmony to all the systems of the body, thus invigorating the entire psychosomatic system of human constitution.

Are the results worth all the effort? The answer is a resounding yes. You will like yourself better and will feel better too. In addition to improved appearance and a new buoyancy, you will have an immeasurable sense of accomplishment, a feeling that you have overcome forces that threatened your peace of mind and physical well-being, and a gratifying sense that you have contributed to the preservation of your life.

Suryanamaskar has many benefits:

- Facilitates weight loss and reduction of paunch.
- Lowers blood pressure.
- Ensures stronger bones and a decreased risk of osteoporosis.
- Elevates levels of 'good' HDL cholesterol.
- Decreases levels of 'bad' LDL cholesterol.
- Decreases levels of triglycerides (fats).
- Increases strength and coordination, which leads to a decrease in the risk of falls.

- Improves sensitivity to insulin.
- Enhances the immune system.
- Causes an overall increase in one's sense of well-being.
- Helps normal functioning of the stomach, bowels and nerve centers, and purifies blood.

One look at this list of health benefits is convincing: any individual who chooses to develop a consistent program of modest exercise is making an important choice to avoid developing many different diseases.

TWO

PRANAYAMA: PRANA OF SURYANAMASKAR

Pranayama is the art of breathing efficiently. This is a vast subject with unlimited potential. My endeavor is that my observations, reflections and experiences will help you achieve precision and refinement in your practice.

Our lungs are wonderful wind bags devised by God. Unfortunately we put immense pressure on them, subjecting them to poor posture, pollution of all kinds such as dust, smoke, industrial fumes, and vehicular emission. Even passive smoking is bad for us. In an average lifetime, our lungs are inflated half a billion times. This kind of wear and tear would destroy any manmade material. Despite the repeated punishment we inflict on these remarkable organs, they give most of us long and trouble-free service!

Wherever we live - in a cold country, arid desert, or polluted city - our lungs require air that is hot, moist, and dust-free. If the smoke and dust we breathe ever reached the lungs' minute air passages, they would be clogged within hours. If bacteria gained free admittance, we would rapidly succumb to infections. It is to guard against such disasters that nature has devised an incredibly complex air-conditioning system in the human body.

The Magic of Deep Breathing

Have you noticed how singers breathe out when they sing, releasing air from the lungs in a moderate and orderly manner? You cannot sing without exhaling gradually, and when you exhale you expel impurities and empty the lungs for a fresh and involuntary intake of air. The same principle is used while practicing *Pranayama* in *Suryanamaskar*, particularly when the mantras are being chanted aloud. This wonderful technique aerates our lungs and removes the stale air from them.

Real breath control means learning to control the way we exhale, not the way we inhale. In this *Suryanamaskar Pranayama*, energy is best renewed by the orderly, disciplined release of breath, not by strenuously pumping the lungs full of air. Orators, singers, swimmers, divers and runners know this. Exhaling helps the body to accommodate itself to change. Careful breath control with emphasis on exhaling helps us to relax under any kind of tension or stress. Most of us are only half-breathers: we breathe in because we cannot help it but we fail to breathe out completely. The result is that we sigh a lot, a sigh of our need to exhale. The sigh is nature's way of deflating the lungs when we have neglected the breathing apparatus long enough. The sensible thing is to learn to sigh in a systematic and organized fashion.

We know that any interference with breathing causes acute distress. It follows that any improvement in breathing creates happiness in the mind and body. Management of breath can tone us up and contribute visibly to our health and vitality. When you inhale, negative pressure is developed in the body and the air comes in; when you exhale, positive pressure is developed and the air goes out in the form of exhalation.

Repeated several times, such exercise makes the body glow with warmth, helping to overcome tenseness, tightness and even depression. This is because you have stimulated your brain and eased the tension with a fuller supply of life-giving oxygen.

One of the main positives gained by breathing out consistently in *Suryanamaskar* exercise is awareness. It introduces a sharp change in our regular habits. Conscious breathing brings with it awareness of posture. You begin to realize that you cannot sit all hunched up and breathe well, either in or out. Automatic breathing is not sufficient for our needs. Sedentary or monotonous work habits call for new and consciously controlled rhythms. Experience will demonstrate the constructive use we can make of a power we tend to overlook.

I strongly believe, and it is also the experience of millions of people all over the world, that deep breathing *Pranayama* in *Suryanamaskar* offers a miraculous system of defense. When you understand a great deal about the human body and its resources for health, you wonder why anyone is ever sick. Like a ship rights herself after keeling over in a storm, the body rights itself after both minor illnesses and major disease. This ability has been called 'the wisdom of the body'.

We actually have a great healing power in ourselves that makes us healthy. Doctors try to imitate and supplement this with medical and surgical work. In our fight against disease we always have this inbuilt powerful force on our side. Health is the thing that makes you feel that *now* is the best time of the year. Natural forces within us are the true healers of disease.

Some of the most dramatic and wonderful things that happen in the human body are the result of its own natural system of defense. Slow, rhythmic deep breathing is probably the single best anti-stress medicine we have. When you bring air down into the lower portion of the lungs voluntarily, where oxygen exchange is most efficient, everything changes. Heart and pulse rate slows, blood pressure decreases, muscles relax, anxiety ceases and the mind calms.

Only a few people know how to breathe correctly. We were taught to suck in our guts and puff out our chest. Females are particularly heavy chest breathers. At the same time, we are bombarded with constant stress, tension and anxiety, which cause muscles to tense and our respiration rate to increase. As a result, we have become a world full of shallow 'chest breathers', using primarily the middle and upper portions of the lungs.

I teach my students the correct way to breathe while performing *Suryanamaskar*, and I have seen breath control alone achieve remarkable results: lowering blood pressure on a day-to-day basis, improving longstanding patterns of poor digestion, decreasing anxiety and allowing people to get rid of addictive anti-anxiety drugs, and improving sleep and energy cycles.

Unlike any other bodily function, breathing is the only one you can do either completely consciously or unconsciously, voluntarily or involuntarily. It is controlled by two different sets of nerves and muscles, voluntary and involuntary. It is the only function through which the conscious mind can influence the involuntary, or autonomic, nervous system, which is responsible for supporting the body in times of crisis. It is like a Super Stress-Buster; just try it once and I am sure you will do it every day.

The rise of stress related disorders and ailments, clinical depression, anxiety, chronic fatigue, insomnia, sleep apnea, etc. is a sign of the times. People are thoroughly indoctrinated by the idea that a certain degree of internal conflicts or war is normal. There is a tendency to internalize feelings, unlike our ancestors who usually had a fight-or-flight response. The lack of physical response to stress can stimulate appetite and encourage fat cells deep inside the abdomen to store what we call 'toxic weight', which many men and women carry around the belly.

Pranayama in Suryanamaskar leads to control of emotions; which in turn brings stability, serenity, concentration and mental poise. It deals with subtle functioning of the breath or the *Prana*, various techniques of inhalation, retention, and exhalation, with unchecked flow through the network of channels *(nadis)* and the subtle centers *(chakras)*. *Pranayama* involves various techniques, which affect and change not only the physical, physiological and neural energies but also the psychological and cerebral activities of the brain, such as memory training and creativity. The invigorating effect on health of *Pranayama in Suryanamaskar,* called voluntary respiration, is beyond words. The multiple effects of such training of mind-body-intellect equipment, not merely on the lungs but on the whole metabolism and chemistry of the human body, are detailed in various textbooks of *Pranayama, such as Shiva-Samhita, Hatha Yoga and Ashtanga Yoga.*

The invisible channels and subtle vessels which flow through the human body are called *nadis*. The channels, through which the psychic energies, like *prana*, flow freely in the human body, are also called *nadis* or the subtle tubular channel of communication. *Nadis* follow the fundamental structure of the body in a similar way as the nerve-system, though they cannot be identified with it, as has often been wrongly maintained. All attempts to prove its presence have only shown that the experiences of yoga cannot be measured with the yardsticks of natural fundamental sciences, physiology and dissecting anatomy, or experimental psychology.

It is difficult to translate the words *prana* or *nadi* as inevitably misunderstandings arise when words like 'nerves', 'arteries', or 'veins' are used. The anatomy and physiology of yoga is not founded on 'object-isolation' investigations or enquires of science, but on self-observation and analysis and on the direct experience of processes and sensations within one's own body.

Like an electric current that freely flows through different means such as iron, water, copper, silver, etc., or moves in the form of radio waves, the current of psychic force, if efficiently concentrated and well directed, can utilize our own breath, or the blood, or the nerves as conductors and at the same time move and act even beyond and without these mediums into the infinity of space. *Prana* is more than the breath, more than nerve-energy or the vital forces within the blood current. It is more than the creative power of semen or the force of motor-nerves, more than the inner faculties of thought and intellect or will-power.

For this reason, the culture of the body and that of the spine is given highest importance and priority in the practice of *Suryanamaskar* on a day-to-day basis.

Again, all methods grouped under yoga are special psychological processes founded on a fixed truth of Nature. The 'organs' which collect, transform and distribute the forces or the powers flowing through them are called *chakras* or centers of force. It is these *chakras* that radiate secondary streams of psychic force, like the spokes of a wheel, the ribs of an umbrella, or the petals of a lotus.

In other words, these *chakras* are such masters in which psychic forces and bodily functions merge into each other. They are the focal points in which cosmic and psychic energies crystallize into bodily qualities, and these bodily qualities are dissolved or transmuted again into psychic forces.

As deep inhalation is done during the *Suryanamskar* work out, the rhythmic up and down movement of the diaphragm massages the abdominal organs evenly, increasing their circulation and efficiency. Changes in coronary flow occur during this type of breathing, allowing more blood to flow into the coronary vessels. The input of healthy blood into the lungs increases, allowing better uptake of oxygen and build up of adenosine triphosphate (ATP) molecules at the cellular level, which is the source of energy to the cell.

Recent evidence points to the role of lifestyle modifications with a special stress on breathing in *Suryanamaskar* and on tranquility of mind as the best insurance against precocious coronary disease. Excellent collateral circulation (natural by-pass) is possible by the devoted practice of *yogasana* and *pranayama*, and it works as a powerful pneumatic tool. The key words are deep and slow breathing. And these techniques have been shown by independent, clinical trials to be effective in increasing lung capacity, reducing the blood plasma levels of cortisol, (the 'stress hormone') and alleviating all sorts of depression, to name a few of the tremendous benefits demonstrated by these studies. *Pranayama* releases layers of stress without effort, removing blocks to the increased energy and joy that are our birthright.

Studies done at our yoga institute show that slowed deep breathing increased tissue perfusion, reduced breathlessness and unstable angina pectoris, made patients get out of bed, reduced the aortic pressure, pulmonary artery pressure, and end diastolic pressure in the left ventricle, and also significantly increased the ejection fraction (LVEF) in patients who were otherwise dying of terminal heart failure. Slow breathing changes many parameters in the heart, makes the mind tranquil and peaceful.

Long ago I began observing the subtle relationships between muscle tissue, nerve fibers, breath and emotions while doing *Suryanamaskar*. It is a great body work technique, integrating multiple levels of body and mind, hardly found in any other exercise. As I become more familiar with the theory and practice of *Suryanamaskar,* I learned to pay attention to the subtle signs of 'body language', and gradually began to see the body as a whole as a reflection or manifestation of the psyche or *chitta* (mind and intellect). It is a very powerful tool for psychotherapy and self-exploration. After relatively short periods of fast, deep breathing, surprisingly intense sensations, related to unconscious emotions and memories will emerge and may trigger a wide range of revealing virgin experiences.

On the other hand, the whole organism of the human body may also undergo a process of self-transformation and self-transcendence, involving stages of crisis and transition, resulting in an entirely new state of 'healthy' balance. It is obvious to me that getting sick and healing are both integral parts of an organism's self-organization.

Deep breathing in *pranayama* makes many changes in the body. It helps to use all the 100% lung capacity, raising the tissue oxygen levels from 40% to 90%. The whole body feels well fed with the life giving oxygen vitality called bio-energy or *prana.* The lowered diaphragm stretches itself to widely open the two holes through which the two great blood vessels *(aorta and inferior vena cava)* taking blood to and from the heart dilate and relax, bringing in less load; simultaneously causing the load on the heart to pump blood out *(preload and after load)* to be significantly reduced, thereby helping the heart to function a lot better. Deep breathing also slows breathing, per force.

Through the ages, men have dreamed of finding a Fountain of Youth; some potion or treatment that would postpone ageing and prolong our useful, vigorous years. *Pranayama* is the answer.

Caution

Attempting to hold your breath forcibly in the lungs, while doing *Suryanamaskar*, is unnatural and decidedly unpleasant. To master deep breathing techniques while doing *Suryanamaskar*, take the help of a qualified yoga teacher.

Vedic and Upanishadic Views of Prana or Bio-Energy

The earth has its own supply of *prana (bio-energy)*, pervading and permeating every atom and every molecule of all the elements and compounds of the Universe. The Sun, a vast reservoir of this unseen vital energy, is constantly pouring an enormous supply of *pranic* radiation on earth as a part of its daily routine. The moon is another big supplier of *prana (bio-energy)* for Mother Earth.

In accordance with the view that the human body is like a universe on a small scale, a microcosm, the polar currents of force which flow through this body are called solar or sun-like and lunar or moon-like forces; acting and affecting the life in the human body 24/7.

According to the scriptural text-books of ancient Bharat, the Sun or *Surya* represents intelligence, the illuminating light of Truth. As this Sun of intelligence is a divine being, the principle of multiplicity in unity, there are many different forms of Sun-Gods, worshipped by different cults and cultures.

Importance of Pranayama (Breathing Techniques) while Doing Suryanamaskar

Each of us seems to be struggling either for peace of mind or fulfillment of desires. With efforts, disciplined behavior and blessings from the Almighty, we will be able to achieve this state of deep and durable satisfaction. Doing *Suryanamaskar* religiously helps to bring a balance between the mind and life.

In *Chandogya Upanishad* there is a wonderful example to illustrate this intimacy between the mind and life - a bird tied to a certain spot with a string tries to fly in all directions but since it cannot fly far, it always comes back to the same spot. This is the state of the human mind which tries to wander everywhere, very rapidly, but not having got shelter anywhere, returns to life and takes refuge there. *Pranayama* of *Suryanamaskar* has a unique place which controls the wandering propensity of the chattering mind.

It is written in the *Bhagwat Gita* that keeping a prosperous body is important while performing this exercise. *Samakaaya Shirogrivam Dhaarayan Achalam Sthiram* - this means that a prosperous body should be measured by the strength of life. Usually, balance does not occur in the human body, but it has been proved worldwide that due to *yogasanas* of *Suryanamaskar*, this equilibrium is achieved easily!

While performing the *pranayama* technique of *Suryanamaskar*, a herculean task takes place in the chest or lungs - inhalation and exhalation. One has to take very deep breaths which results in the expansion of the chest and while breathing out exhalation also takes place to the fullest, throwing impure air out of every nook and corner of the lungs. The resultant outcome is that the human excretory system and all other important organs of the body function effectively.

The body is the true wealth of humans. It is made up of five elements - earth, fire, water, air and sky - known as *Pancha-Taatvas* or five principles. The body is the temple of the soul. Our physical organs of action and our five sense organs (organs of perception) are the pillars of the above mentioned five elements of the human body. Is it not then our responsibility to take care of the well-being of this pure human body physically as well as mentally?

THREE

THE BACKBONE OF YOUR LIFE

The human skeleton is a tell-tale index of health and a marvel of engineering. For most people a chair is a place to relax and be comfortable but in reality it is more important to see that the framework of your body is supported by that chair. Doing *Suryanamaskar* every day ensures that your back and other muscles are kept in optimum condition.

Most bad backs are self-inflicted, and are second only to headaches as a source of bodily misery and pain. Back trouble can be of different kinds: lumbago, ruptured discs, sacroiliacs, slipped vertebrae, wrenched muscles, torn ligaments, hunched back and ankiolosis. The problem is almost always caused due to misuse or overuse of the back. Pushing, lifting, pulling and all forms of stooping and twisting account for their share one way or the other. Poor postural habits in standing, sitting or sleeping often result in a chronic bad back.

There is no such thing as a 'lazy bone' in your body. They are among the busiest living organs in the body, thriving manufacturing plants which make red and white blood cells 24 hours a day. Every minute, about 180,000,000 red cells die, never to be seen again. But your bones must replace them with healthy young cells, or you face anemic death. It takes six to eight weeks for the marrow to restore the red blood cells after a pint of blood has been removed. Bones have other major duties; they produce the white blood cells which fight off infection as well as the platelets which are essential for blood clotting, and they act as one of the body's warehouses for reserve nourishment. The marrow stores fats and proteins for the time of need. If the calcium supply for the blood, nerves and muscles is lower than normal, the body withdraws some from the skeleton bank.

If you spend your days in an armchair, your system assumes that you have no need for strong bones and proceeds to remove part of the precious minerals slowly. Thus, people who fail to exercise are much more likely to suffer disabling fractures in their later years of life. Our bones are among the most durable objects on earth. Human bones have been found that are nearly a million years old. Bones do not dissolve in water; if they did, they would soon be washed away by the body fluids. Hence, they can outlast iron and other metals affected by dampness.

Each component part of the skeleton is tailored to a specific job or assignment. The spine even has its own built-in shock absorbers - the discs of cushioning cartilage between segments.

The leg bones are hollow in nature, in keeping with the engineering principles that a hollow column is stronger than a solid one of equal weight. On a weight-for-weight basis bones are stronger than steel. Bone construction is comparable to reinforced cement concrete. Bones contain thousands of small blood vessels and are quite as much alive as one's stomach. Active little cells called osteoblasts work day and night, manufacturing new bone, while house-wrecking cells known as osteoclasts labor just as hard tearing down material tagged for the scrap heap. All the long bones grow from maturation areas, or 'centers', by the addition of calcium and other materials and minerals. The 23 bones of the skull are separated by divisions called 'sutures'. As age advances, these sutures disappear one after the other, according to a rigorous schedule.

By watching your step, particularly when you are anxious, angry or tense, you can help keep your faithful skeleton from something it doesn't deserve - a bad back. And by practicing *Suryanamaskar*, you will keep your skeleton and shock-absorber healthy and elastic.

The Miracles of Muscles

It is a law of nature that unless particular groups of muscles are exercised vigorously, they undergo a process of wasting and gradually become less and less efficient for the performance of their intended functions. So either use them or lose them.

It is best, of course, not to wait until muscles are weakened before giving them the care and consideration they deserve. For, to a great degree, we are what our muscles make us - sick or well, vigorous or droopy, alive or dead.

Physiologists say that one reason people are touchy, easily insulted or grieved, is that they go through life with jaws set, faces strained and muscles tense. This causes them to jump at the slightest noise or the slightest insult to their egos. It is not their nerves on edge, but it is their muscles, from eyelids to toes, that are reacting. When all the muscles are relaxed and at ease, then your nerves and ego will also be at ease.

Muscle or flesh is composed of microscopic cells, some what the shape of an elongated cigar. Each muscle cell is just like a muscle in miniature. When a muscle contracts, it becomes harder and shorter, but its total bulk does not alter. Muscles never act singly, a group or groups of muscles are involved in the simplest movements which one can easily feel or notice in any movement or exercise.

Much as been written about the indefatigable muscles of the heart. Exercises designed by our ancient *yogis* take every care of all cardiac (heart) muscles which pump almost 8,000 liters of blood every 24 hours. *Suryanamaskar* makes these muscles, strong, supple and elastic, helping to extend one's life-span too.

We speak of 'muscles of iron'. Yet in reality the working or contractile, element in muscle is a soft jelly. It is this jelly that contracts to lift a thousand times its own weight that is truly a miracle of the universe. All types of muscles are efficient machines for converting chemical energy (food) into mechanical energy (work).

There is a great deal all of us can do to keep our muscles functioning well. First, they must be properly fed. Generally speaking, the average diet includes all the protein needed for muscle repair and all the carbohydrate required for muscle fuel. But muscles can starve through lack of exercise - witness hospital patients who eat perfectly balanced meals and get out of bed too weak to walk. In the sedentary adult, a large number of these capillaries are collapsed, out of business, nearly all the time. Exercise alone can open them up and provide better muscle nutrition.

Often, muscles get fatigued when required to work at too fast a rate. One housewife rushes through her chores and is worn out by noon, while another more leisurely one accomplishes just as much and finishes the day still fresh. All work and exercise should be paced to get the most out of our muscles. Like all other body organs and tissues, muscles too must have rest. Millions of people sleep the traditional eight hours and then get up exhausted. The most likely explanation: one set of muscles has been cramped, tensed all night, wearing out the rest of the body. The best way to avoid this is to lie quietly in bed, legs straight and arms at the side. Contract one set of muscles at a time, and consciously relax them.

When the nutritional reserve in the muscle has been drained through overuse or exercise of the muscle, then, during the post exercise stiffness period, chilling can result in protracted spasms. It is important therefore after vigorous exercise to take a hot shower or a hot bath and get warm; this has a tremendous impact on your muscles.

One of the objectives of *Suryanamaskar* is to mobilize the spinal segment and to correct the postural distortion, to strengthen the extensor muscles of the back and the muscles of the shoulder blades and to develop the pectoral muscles. The fast movements and quick change in different positions ensure freedom of movement, creating agility and flexibility while it improves blood circulation. The dull brain becomes active and the brooding mind gets refreshed. In this exercise, the trunk and the torso are the center of attention; the will is concentrated upon the movements of its most motile and motivated area; while the limbs of locomotion play a subsidiary part. The immediate result is that the flow of blood rushes through the network of large blood vessels, lessening rather than increasing the blood pressure slightly; the heart's action is stimulated instead of being impeded, the breathing is deepened and prolonged, and a feeling of exhilaration and buoyancy takes the place of tumultuous heart action and distressed breathing. At the same time, the bowels are stimulated and educated by the kneading and squeezing to which they are subjected by the actively contracting and relaxing abdominal muscles.

Poor, sloppy, misaligned standing postures lead to disorders of the spine, hips, knees, and of the internal organs. Added to this, we may have stiff lumber and cervical muscles, tight hamstring muscles or over flexible muscles, which result in postural pain or postural defects.

To correct all this and avoid future problems, our ancient *yogis* have prescribed *Suryanamaskar* to maintain the health of the locomotor system. To gain the desired end, therefore, *Suryanamaskar* has to be done systematically and scientifically. It must be so performed as to develop and strengthen almost every part of the body.

In one way or other, the failure of muscles to contract properly accounts for the vast majority of deaths - from heart failure, high blood pressure and other diseases. Hence, the importance of *Suryanamaskar* exercise in daily life.

FOUR

THE FAT FACTOR

Extra fat is like a punishment to the body. Excessive deposit of fat around the belly, or anywhere in the body, is a departure from health; it points to a loss of balance between intake of nutrients and their consumption. The local deposition of fat interferes with the many fundamental functions of the vital organs that are embedded in it; for example, the heart muscle is weakened, the abdominal viscera are weighed down, respiration is taxed, and the protuberant belly hides overweight feet. Proper habits in both food and exercise can help a person avoid these problems.

Fat can adversely affect your health and active years. In India, decrease in physical activity with increasing age aggravates the problem. The percentage of obese people is increasing at an alarming rate. Obesity is likely to emerge as the single most significant public health problem in India a decade from now.

The term obesity implies a disease of excessive accumulation of body fat. The emphasis is on 'disease' and 'body fat', not excess weight. You may be overweight but you may not be obese - yet. In order to find the level at which excess weight becomes harmful, it is necessary to quantify obesity. The best way to do this is to calculate your Body Mass Index (BMI). BMI is calculated by dividing a person's weight in kilograms with the square of their height in meters.

It is often said that after the age of 40 'men put on weight in front, and women behind'. This is the inevitable result of excessive drinking, eating the wrong kind of food, and lack of exercise. It is equally true that by taking suitable exercise anyone can reduce a good deal from one's total weight, and thus add to their general well-being.

It's All in the Family

New research says obese fathers have overweight children. Over the last few centuries conventional wisdom cautioned pregnant women against indulging in unhealthy habits. Expectant and nursing mothers were supposed to eat certain foods and generally maintain a worry-free life. In recent times, modern medicine has added a few more things to this list, advancing the responsibility to well before women become pregnant. But there was no such advice for fathers, as it was thought that they had no role in the health of their offspring.

It is increasingly becoming clear that fathers who smoke are risking disease in their offspring in later life. Smoking is known to cause genetic changes in the sperm, and these changes lead to many diseases in children which can continue well into adulthood. This finding has not surprised anybody, as the dangers of smoking are well accepted. Recent research from the University of Adelaide throws up a surprising finding: obese fathers have obese and sick children, and this effect can last at least for two generations. It does not seem to matter how healthy the children's lifestyles are, if their father is obese they will suffer the consequences.

When a man becomes obese, it leads to changes in the micro RNA of the sperm. Micro RNA regulates gene expression and so is an extremely important part of the cell machinery. The changes in micro RNA can lead to the programming of the embryo for obesity throughout life. It also leads to other metabolic changes in children that can result in Type II diabetes, not just in the child but in their offspring as well.

A good waistline is obtainable even after 40 years of age. Diminished waist measurement will mean increasing fitness and improved body condition. This will result in a brighter mental outlook and better capacity to work. The muscles of the abdomen play a very important part when we determine the overall health of a person. Exercise helps to train lateral muscles of the stomach, transversals and external and internal obliques. It has a great effect on the blood supply to the abdominal organs. The pump like action during *Suryanamaskar* relieves the stagnation which tends to frequently occur in the blood stream there. By its stimulating effect on the bowels it improves their tone and thus helps to counteract any tendency to chronic or acute constipation.

Strong wrists and forearms are of great assistance no doubt, but the real seat of power lies in the loins and abdomen. At the same time, mere muscular strength does not mean physical fitness. Health and fitness do not depend on your arms and legs, the limbs of locomotion; they are more dependent on your chest and abdomen.

Take care of this first. It is actually the lower abdomen, where the greatest weight rests, that is the point of greatest stress.

FIVE

SUNSHINE AND VITAMIN D

We all know the usual prescription for good health — a balanced diet with lots of fruits and vegetables, combined with regular exercise. Now add, spending time in the sun to this list.

Till recently, we were always warned that excessive exposure to the Sun resulted in wrinkles, age spots, and the increasing threat of skin cancer. But new studies suggest that sunlight is actually beneficial for us. The

Vitamin D it prompts our bodies to make may prevent cancer, protect against heart disease and ward off a long list of disorders such as multiple sclerosis, rheumatoid arthritis, diabetes and gum disease. Vitamin D is vitally important for bone building; it is needed for calcium absorption. Almost every tissue and cell in the body has receptors for Vitamin D, which means that every tissue and cell needs Vitamin D to function maximally.

According to a study carried out by WHO, a person with a deficiency of Vitamin D easily falls prey to mental and physical ailments. Doctors attribute the rising trend of deficiency to changing lifestyles and low dietary calcium, combined with the Indian skin color. An increasing number of children who spend long hours indoors complain about aches and pains, symptomatic of Vitamin D deficiency. The nutrient that is best sourced from sun rays, not only helps strengthen bones and teeth and build immunity, but also helps prevent auto-immune disorders, infections and the risk of developing cancers.

How Suryanamaskar Helps

Sunlight is an integral part of our lives. And we are so fortunate that this life giving gift of sunlight is available to us free of cost. There can be no better radiation than the rays of the morning sun! The energy, light and power (strength) that we receive from the sun helps us to lead an enriched life.

Performing *Suryanamaskar* early in the morning helps our bodies to absorb this life giving solar energy.

During *Suryanamaskar*, the sun's rays collide with our thoughts and create silence. The photons from the sun enter the pineal gland located at the base of the skull. It acts as the body's light meter, receiving light activated information from the eyes (by way of the hypothalamus) and then sending out hormonal messages that have a profound effect on the mind and the body. It synchronizes the information with the external environment through secretion of hormones. The pineal gland which is photon sensitive is activated by the light coming through the eyes, producing a hormone call Serotonin which stimulates other glands, to lower blood pressure, increase body metabolism and help control the mind. When the pineal gland does not receive sunlight, it secrets another hormone called Melatonin which induces sleep, increases blood sugar and a craze for food, leading to obesity, fears and anxiety.

SIX

A SENSIBLE DIET

It has been said that half of the people in the world are on diet and the other half are starving!

Doctors agree that a majority of people eat too much and too often. Most people fail to understand the elementary principles of a proper diet. A moderate well chewed meal will give more energy than a heavy meal hastily swallowed. Proper chewing of food is very important as digestion starts in the mouth. It is not the amount we gulp, but rather what we digest that nourishes us.

Most people who put on weight are sedentary workers who consume too much food, especially sugar, starches and alcohol. Excessive weight can be reduced by daily exercise, but no amount of exercise permits overeating of fat-forming 'fat' food. Worrying and hurrying while eating leads to problems of digestion. Effects of this can also be seen in liver derangement, sluggish bowel action with much flatulence, nervous irritability, sleeplessness or sometimes breathlessness, and elevated blood pressure levels. For men over 40 this is almost axiomatic.

People who say they have no time to chew their food properly and do a few minutes of regular exercise usually end up constipated. The time they waste trying to relieve their bowels would have been better used doing the necessary chewing, and practicing an exercise like *Suryanamaskar* to stir up the sluggish contents of their abdomen.

Many businessmen want to get well, but without changing the habits that have made them ill; and those who say that they have no time to remain fit, usually find time to get sick.

We have to pay a heavy price for the neglect of our bodies, for over-indulgence and laziness. Instead, for a small amount of time and trouble we can have an efficient body, an alert mind, sharpness of intellect, and a general feeling of wellness.

Most people expect a hasty breakfast and then a quick lunch to carry them through the eleven hours during which the mind and body are working at top speed. They have a big meal in the evening to compensate for what they should have had during the day. During the night while sleeping, the body transforms the food mainly into fat, and not useful energy.

Most women today seem to have the idea that skipping meals is an easy way to reduce weight and generally improve their appearance. Nothing could be further from the truth. Insufficient intake of the vitamins and minerals after exercise is likely to cause anemia, in which the blood thins, the skin may become sallow and rough, the complexion suffers from pimples and sores, and circles develop under the eyes.

Medical surveys indicate that skipping breakfast or eating too little doesn't go with the practice of *Suryanamaskar* as an exercise. Breakfast is the most important meal of the day, and skipping it results in a noticeable loss of efficiency at work, ill health, many industrial accidents and much irritability.

There is no excuse for a skimpy breakfast. With automatic cooking apparatus, conveniently packaged and scientifically enriched breakfast foods and cereals, frozen fruits and fruit juices, breakfast should not be a chore to make. Eat three moderate meals a day, with emphasis on breakfast. Save part of what you would normally eat at lunch or dinner for snack time; then you can nibble without adding more calories.

A Small Waistline is a Long Life Line

A person who can reduce (and remain like that) has to be strongly motivated to embark on a lifetime plan involving new habits. Family members play an important role in this. In many cases, the motivation is fear. The death rate for overweight people is higher than for those of normal weight. The decision to reduce weight literally should be a matter of life and death. It should not be a source of misery in the first place. Since overeating is the basic cause of overweight in most cases, the first step in any program is to determine why you overeat. Emotional needs, feelings of inadequacy, disappointment and anger often makes people seek solace in food.

Once you face the reasons for your overeating, they lose much of their hold on you. Boredom and frustration also lead to overeating. Coordinating your weight-loss program with a change in your way of life can provide satisfaction formerly relieved by food. Try a new pursuit like gardening, playing a sport or even engaging in minor odd jobs at home. Seek help with your plan, from your spouse or if you are younger, your parents. A good family doctor is an invaluable asset, one who is willing to help you explore your emotional as well as physical needs.

Changing your food patterns should not be difficult. I am opposed to rigid, printed diets, one-food diets, calorie-counting devices, weight-reducing *tamashas* and gimmicks of all kinds. What you weigh now is most likely the result of your long-term eating patterns. Short-term crash diets are always unsuccessful. The key to successful weight control is to remember that it must be a life-long activity, of which you are constantly aware.

It is difficult to suddenly change basic eating patterns of many years' standing, so don't alter your eating habits too drastically. Losing a few kilos and then regaining them after sometime means that you have relapsed into your old habits. It is better to slowly adapt to a new plan which you can stick to.

Remember to eat slowly. When you take your time, savoring each morsel, the appetite is more readily appeased than it is when you gulp down food.

Fatigue gives you an abnormal appetite but never eat too much when you are over tired. Instead of the quick pick-me-up you are after, the meal is likely to lie undigested and can cause gastric complications. If you are carrying around extra weight, whether it's a load of cement or fat, you are putting more work on your heart. For fat persons I advise 'scientific nibbles'— a small bite in the morning and afternoon of some food that you ordinarily would have at lunch or at supper.

Weight is determined by the number of calories you put into the body machine balanced against the number you expend. The important thing to remember is that energy expenditure every day, every week, every year will make a difference in the long run. To make physical activity pay, stay with it for life.

What is a Healthy Diet?

Diet is the base for our good health. Each one of us needs to decide on our daily diet, ensuring that it provides the required number of calories, necessary amino acids, appropriate amounts of saturated fats, omega three and omega six fatty acids and dissolvable and un-dissolvable fiber. A scientifically pure and balanced diet should be formulated based on personal preferences, economic capability, age, nature and time of work, genetic illnesses, height, weight, and availability of food.

Breakfast time should ideally be between 8 and 9 am. This is when you must eat sumptuously, like a king, as the digestion is most effective during this time. Then, between 1 and 2 pm one should have light lunch which must include salads and curds or buttermilk. Dinner should be had early, say between 7 and 8 pm and it should be light. There should be a gap of at least two hours before going to bed.

People who eat a low-fat diet, which includes at least three servings of fruits and vegetables daily, enjoy a lot of health benefits, such as:

- Weight loss.
- A decreased risk of diabetes.
- A decreased risk of heart disease.
- A decreased risk of almost all cancers.
- A decreased risk of high blood pressure.
- A decreased risk of elevated cholesterol.
- An enhanced immune system.
- An increased sensitivity to insulin.
- Increased energy and ability to concentrate.

Yogic Diet Dos and Don'ts

It is exceedingly important to be aware of what we must eat to ensure a healthy mind and body connection.

- Avoid or try to limit the intake of hot beverages like tea and coffee.
- Stay away from tobacco, drugs and alcohol.
- Consume fatty foods, milk products like cottage cheese, *mawa*, sweets, and non-vegetarian food in small quantities.
- Ensure that your daily diet has less salt, sugar and refined flour (*maida*).
- Include at least 300 ml. of milk in your breakfast, taking into consideration the age and constitution of the body.
- Soak 4 to 5 almonds overnight and eat them first thing in the morning.

- Have at least two helpings of seasonal fruit every day. You can have milk with *chikkoo* and banana but avoid a mixed fruit salad, which may result in acidity.
- Consume sprouts, leafy vegetables, all types of beans, vegetables, and raw salads in large quantities.
- Regularly eat *khichadi* made of rice and pulses.
- Avoid having curds or buttermilk at night.
- Drink a glass of water an hour before meals; do not consume water in between meals or at least until one hour later.
- Ensure that your daily diet contains 15% fats, 35% proteins, and 50% carbohydrates. The daily meal should comprise *chapattis*, rice, vegetables, pulses and salads.
- Always have freshly cooked food; avoid food stored in the refrigerator for a long time.
- Eat food items like sweets or fried food sparingly. Overeating can cause stress to the digestive system and result in indigestion.
- If you suffer from hyper-acidity, eat light food 3 to 4 times a day.
- Drink plenty of water.
- Try to reduce sodium salt intake and add black or rock salt to your daily diet; however do not completely stop salt intake as it contains Iodine.

SEVEN

SURYANAMASKAR FOR WOMEN

The three landmark phases in any woman's life are the start of periods (age of menarche), childbirth, and menopause. Women have benefitted tremendously by doing *Suryanamaskar* during all these three phases. Medical science and gynecology have advanced by leaps and bounds, but there can be no substitute for the right exercise, yoga and a balanced diet.

As women get older, their metabolic rate reduces, so by the time they reach their forties, they tend to gain weight. Around the same time their menopausal stage also sets in. This results in weight gain, mood swings, identity crisis, hormonal imbalance, and all this has a major impact on the psyche of the women. They start feeling suffocated and get disenchanted with life. At such times, the family members, husband or children have an important role to play; they must try to understand what she is going through and help her through this difficult time. Practicing *Suryanamaskar* in this critical phase encourages blood circulation and helps in balancing hormones.

The truth is, whether male or female, after 35, the ageing process in the body begins. How much ever one tries, health issues start cropping up around this time. Women need more flexibility as compared to strength in their daily household chores at this stage of life. Similarly, they need to increase the capacity of their pelvic and uterine muscles. Engaging in regular exercise, *yogasanas* and *Suryanamaskar* helps proper circulation of blood, and menstrual cramps and other related complaints can be reduced. The internal glands of the body will remain active; this has a bearing on the mind, which in turn will make life more meaningful for the woman.

Puberty

Stepping into puberty brings about different emotional, physical and biological changes. The mind witnesses new ideas and emotions. The onset of menstruation is normally between the ages of 11 to 14 years. The limbs and bones start developing in a typical way. The body is being prepared for its ultimate task of reproduction. This is the right time to introduce *Suryanamaskar* into the daily routine. Many young girls find menstruation a pain or a nuisance; working on physical fitness and mental strength can help to deal with this.

During the menstruation cycle doing physically strenuous work is not advisable. It is also very important to keep the mind balanced and stable. If one does proper pelvic girdle exercises during this period, the muscles in the pelvic area become strong and blood circulation improves, which results in minimal discomfort. Food or supplements rich in calcium, Vitamin C, iron, etc. help increase the hemoglobin in the blood. The blood flow during the menstrual cycle and its amount depends on hormones like estrogens and progesterone.

Preparing the body for Child-bearing

Before conceiving, a woman should visit a doctor to rule out any problems. Only when the doctor has confirmed that she is fit and fine should she take up *Suryanamaskar* or any other similar exercise. She should also seek guidance from a dietician who can help put her on the right path where food is concerned. Childhood disorders and genetic ailments can be well managed with appropriate care, medication and food.

A healthy fetus depends on various factors such as the time of conception, the state of the uterus, pelvic muscles, spine, ovum, ovaries, and male sperm. Regular exercise such as *Suryanamaskar* is very important at this time to allow the body to degenerate proportionately. The biggest advantage of this is that the woman's capacity to bear pain while in labor increases considerably. The leg muscles become strong and back problems are kept under control.

Post-delivery Care

World over, gynecologists have been advising women to exercise post-delivery. This is a time to become active - to recoup from all the degeneration that has taken place in the body. This is when the body rejuvenates and gets re-engineered. However, after childbirth, it is important to have an exercise schedule which does not need too much practice or training. Consult your attending doctor before opting for a brisk walk every alternate day, and performing as many *Suryanamaskars* as possible. Child birth is a natural process and it is beneficial if one brings about some changes in the daily routine during this time.

Advantages of *Suryanamaskar* for nursing mothers:

- Ensures lasting physical and mental fitness.
- Controls weight gain, if any.
- Aids smooth movements and reduces imbalance of the body.

However, some words of caution:

- Do not exercise in excess or too vigorously.
- Drink enough water to maintain the hydration level of the body; the color of the urine should be like that of water.
- Wear loose and comfortable clothing.
- Maintain a balanced, nutritious and proportionate diet; reduce sodium and salt intake.
- Make sure that the muscles, especially around the abdomen and pelvis, are not over stressed.
- Ensure there is minimal stress on the joints. Make it a habit to stand straight; sitting posture should be erect.
- Chew your food well.
- Sleep on a flat and hard bed and take enough rest.
- Avoid bending while working.
- Keep the mind happy and entertained.

Hormonal Changes During Menopause

In the forties, the level of estrogens and progesterone hormones reduces drastically and menopause normally sets in. This impacts the mind and body, sometimes adversely. The skin becomes dry, dull and lifeless; it loses its suppleness and starts sagging. Some women have considerable physical discomfort during the changeover. The commonest symptom is the 'hot flushes' which are caused by hormonal imbalance. The bones also become weak and brittle; a small misstep can fracture them. Lack of sleep, headaches, fatigue, and a sense of feeling miserable and irritable are common.

Along with the physical effects, one must also pay attention to the mental aspect in menopausal women. There are terrible mood swings. This is usually a time in the woman's life, especially if she is a housewife, when she is facing other changes like children leaving home, or busy with school or college, and husbands busy in their careers; she tends to feel a strong sense of worthlessness and loneliness.

All these physiological as well as psychological changes are natural and there are remedies for them. Regular exercise can help in curtailing the ill effects of menopause. It is advisable to start doing *yogasanas* coupled with *Suryanamaskar* under the guidance of an expert in the field. Care must be taken to do the exercise gradually and within limits.

Suryanamaskar exercise has a wonderful effect on the skin at such times. The thyroid glands in the neck become more efficient and the result is felt all over the body. Likewise, the pituitary glands too help produce hormones. The mantras chanted while doing *Suryanamaskar* and *Pranayam* bring about positive changes and elevate the mood. A lasting sense of joy prevails! *Shavasan* or 'yogic sleep' done after performing *Suryanamaskar* helps in overcoming feelings of lethargy, irritation, fatigue, low self-esteem, indigestion, etc.

Suryanamaskar is a natural tonic which energizes, refreshes and strengthens the body and mind. Doing *Suryanamaskar* provides the mental and physical strength needed to face this period of life and helps make the transition smooth and effortless.

EIGHT

SURYANAMASKAR AND THE HEART

Look around and you will see many people suffering from conditions like diabetes, high blood pressure and/or heart related problems. India will soon earn the dubious distinction of having the highest number of patients suffering from diabetes, hypertension, heart related ailments, and obesity! By 2015 it will also boast of the maximum number of patients suffering from depression.

These diseases have become so common the world over, cutting across age, class, color and creed! Heart problems can afflict anyone from a youngster in the 20s to pensioners. Heart specialists from the western world call this epidemic 'the Indian paradox' - just like one inherits one's father's property, one also inherits the disease! The American medical fraternity has nicknamed this the 'widow maker disease'!

Central Obesity or Syndrome X has become a global phenomenon, especially among children. The need for physical fitness must be stressed right from the early school days; *Suryanamaskar* should be made a mandatory part of a fitness routine even for children so that they do not fall prey to lifestyle diseases in their 30s.

Capacity of the Heart

While testing the fitness of the heart, we observe how effectively the body uses the oxygen. The capacity or fitness level of sportspersons is generally tested by using an Ergometer to conduct the VO2 max test. The VO2 max level goes down or reduces as we age. Heredity also plays a role here.

Here is a table indicating VO2-Max:

VO2 Max	Age
47.7	25
43.1	35
39.5	45
34.5	60

Along with oxygen, the fuel of the body, heartbeats per minute also tell us about the fitness of the body. As age increases, maximum heart rate comes down.

Heart Rate	Age
180-200	20
150-270	30
140-160	50

I have not mentioned the heart rate after the age of 50 years because at that age, the heart rate varies from person to person. Regular habit of doing *Suryanamaskar* helps in maintaining the pulse and heart rate appropriate to that age group by strengthening the muscles of the heart.

Sports physiologists and cardiologists have proved that moderate-regular-intense activity-in which body temperature and heart beats rise a little bit and you tax your cardio-respiratory system to the point where you may puff out a bit but not uncontrollably, is superbly and incredibly beneficial when it comes to preventing and curing obesity, heart disease and diabetes, which are killer diseases.

NINE

CHILDREN AND SURYANAMASKAR

It has been observed that children who connect with nature and exercise regularly perform better in school, exhibit fewer behavioral challenges, and experience fewer attention-deficit disorders. We need to ensure that our young generation explores and reveres nature, enjoys life outdoors, and exercises regularly. The instinct to connect with the outdoors tends to get buried, the older we get. We have to ensure that children remain totally in touch with the incredible web of life around them.

Children today tend to spend more time indoors glued to some gadget or the other instead of expending energy outdoors. The problem of lack of exercise has resulted in childhood obesity becoming a global problem. It is also becoming a serious health problem in India, where the childhood obesity rate is about 22%, and increasing every year.

We need to arrest the physical degeneration of our youth before the adverse effects on their health and wellbeing have a chance to set in. Intelligence and skill can function at peak levels only when the body is healthy and strong. Schools do not need specialized gym facilities; short work outs are possible even in the school yard or the classroom itself.

Consumption of junk food is one of the main reasons for obesity among children. Another culprit is fructose, an extremely dangerous and addictive substance widely found in many processed foods which can lead to serious health problems. Children must be fed a balanced, nutritious diet, which combined with regular exercise, will keep them physically fit and mentally alert.

Suryanamaskar should be incorporated as part of the physical education curriculum in schools. It has been proven that *Suryanamaskar* helps reduce weight, brings down blood pressure, and lowers sugar levels in the blood. Children can start doing the exercise from the age of nine years.

SURYANAMASKAR AND CHILDHOOD DISEASES

Hypertension and Weight

High blood pressure and weight are closely related. Peer pressure and stress of studies may lead to weight gain, high blood pressure, and diabetes among children. These conditions are increasingly being detected, especially among teenagers.

Overweight children, when they reach their thirties, are highly prone to high blood pressure, diabetes, heart problems and other ailments. If these overweight children reduce their weight, blood pressure will come down by 2 millimeters for every 1.5 kg weight reduction. BMI or body mass index is another parameter to check weight. If the BMI is between 18 and 24 then the weight is considered to be appropriate. It is very easy to calculate the BMI - simply divide the weight in kilograms by height in meters. *Suryanamaskar*, coupled with an appropriate and balanced diet, helps to maintain the BMI within levels.

Diabetes

Modernization and industrialization have no doubt made our lives easier but it has sadly brought along some side effects and even school kids have not been spared. More and more children are falling prey to Juvenile Diabetes. The main reason for this is inadequate diet, lack of exercise and a sedentary lifestyle. Formerly, cycling or walking to school was common as was spending hours playing outdoor games. These days the routine of children is so different! They are driven to school; outdoor games are minimal; watching TV and playing on the computer has increased; and eating junk food with colas is common. This inactivity invites obesity and juvenile diabetes.

To add to their woes, they are under constant parental pressure to perform well and score high marks. There is an unhealthy race to score higher than XYZ! Not surprising, the blood sugar levels rise; this also results in weight gain. If the abdominal region increases, the fat around the pancreas also increases. As a result, the pancreas is unable to produce enough insulin, resulting in the children taking medicine for diabetes. Parents need to understand that diabetes may become a lifelong problem for their children. An ailment like diabetes can create many complications in our body.

Regular exercise like *Suryanamaskar* not only increases strength, stamina and endurance, but also burns plenty of calories, which in turn reduce fats and cholesterol. One can do approximately 20 *Suryanamaskar* in just 10 minutes. This means one can do around 175 *yogasanas* in these 20 *Suryanamaskars*! Consequently, the energy released from fats goes on increasing as they are burned. In this manner harmful fat accumulated around the abdomen, which leads to heart disorders and diabetes, gets utilized and this results in keeping the blood sugar levels perfectly under control.

Heart Problems

Those youngsters and children who have heart related problems or asthma, or have a family history of hereditary illnesses, should embark on the *Suryanamaskar* exercise regime only after a complete medical consultation and check-up. It has been observed that in some hereditary diseases there are no outward symptoms. Children born with a weak heart or a heart defect, or suffering from high blood pressure or high pulse rate must refrain from doing *Suryanamaskar* unless they have their doctor's go ahead.

Caution

Just doing *Suryanamaskar* is not enough to keep diabetes, heart problems and obesity at bay; one needs to combine this exercise routine with a balanced and healthy diet under expert supervision.

Focusing the Mind

Suryanamaskar increases the capability of the mind,

intelligence and sense organs. In this competitive world, it is very important to have good concentration and good memory to face the many challenges and stress.

Let's take the example of the magnifying glass. Just by focusing on a single ray of the sun, the magnifying glass can burn anything within a fraction of a second. Likewise, if our mind gets focused, it can prove to be of immense strength.

The chanting of mantras while practicing *Suryanamaskar* also helps make children emotionally, intellectually, and physically strong, equipping them to handle stress.

If we are able to inculcate the values of performing such exercise in our children right from their school years, and make it an integral part of their daily routine, they will learn to handle all kinds of stress with ease.

TEN

THE MIRACLE MANTRAS

A 'mantra' is defined by the dictionary as a word or sound repeated to aid concentration in meditation. Coming from the Sanskrit word '*man*' or think, related to the word mind, it literally means thought behind speech or action. Mantras are a combination of syllables, sounds, or phrases, which can be chanted or sung, used as an object of concentration and embodying some aspect of spiritual power. *Omkar* and *Gayatri* are two of the most powerful mantras.

Looking after the sanctity of our human body, a temple created by God, should become a spiritual endeavor that is of utmost importance. *Suryanamaskar* is a well balanced combination of yoga postures that keeps the body and mind healthy. While doing the *Suryanamaskar* specific mantras are sung in praise of the Sun. Chanting mantras extends benefits that have a subtle yet penetrating effect on both the mind and the body.

First begin with a *shloka* to Lord Narayan:

> *Dhyeyahsadasavutramandalmadhyarthi*
> *Narayanahsarsijasansannivishthana*
> *Keyurwaanammakarkundalwaanamkiriti*
> *Haarihiranmayawapurdhatshakhchakraha*

The above *shloka* means that one should always worship Lord *Narayan* who is described as one who exists in the galaxy, in a sitting posture, wearing an armlet and earrings in the shape of a ram, a crown, and a floral garland; conch and a chakra in the hand; and a body that has a blinding glow like gold.

> *Aadidevnamastubhyampraseedmambhaskara*
> *Divaakarnamastubhyamprabhakarnamostute*

The first and foremost God, *Suryanarayana*, I bow down to you with folded hands. You are the God of life, please be happy with me and bless me Oh Lord *Diwakar*. Please accept my salutations to you the bright God.

Say this *shloka* before doing *Suryanamskar*. Then chant the 13 mantras which are different names of the Sun God and begin the exercise. As you perform the steps of *Suryanamaskar*, you should simultaneously chant the following 13 mantras of the Sun God:

1. Om Mitraaya Namah
2. Om Ravaye Namah
3. Om Suryaya Namah
4. Om Bhanve Namah
5. Om Khagaya Namah
6. Om Pushne Namah
7. Om Hiranyagarbhaya Namah
8. Om Marichye Namah
9. Om Adityaya Namah
10. Om Savinnay Namah
11. Om Arkaaya Namah
12. Om Bhaskaraya Namah
13. Om Shri Savitra Surya Narayanaya Namah

HOW TO DO SURYANAMASKAR

Suryanamaskar can be an excellent aerobic exercise. Apart from all the physical benefits, it also boosts morale, maintains good mental health and boosts peace of mind. What is important however is to do the exercise correctly.

Before we incorporate this exercise method in our daily routine, it is imperative we keep certain things in mind.

- Sleep on time so that you can wake up early enough to do *Suryanamaskar*. Try and get at least six and a half hours of sleep.
- As soon as you get up, rub both your palms together; then gently rub the palms over your face. The motion created by rubbing the palms will remove lethargy and the energy produced due to friction makes one feel fresh and active. This is called a palming exercise.
- At night, place some water in a copper utensil; the next morning, heat the water till it is lukewarm and drink at least two glasses. This cleanses the stomach and encourages bowel movements. Always make sure that the stomach is empty before you do *Suryanamaskar*.
- Bathe and wear loose fitting clothes that allow the sun's rays to fall on the body.
- Do not wear any footwear while doing *Suryanamaskar*.
- Find a convenient place to do this exercise, may be in front of a window, on the terrace, or in the garden or any open space.
- Face east while doing *Suryanamaskar*, so that the sun's rays fall on you.
- Place a mat, blanket, rug or sack cloth under the feet.
- Do the exercise with a focused mind.
- Perform each step very carefully and slowly initially.

Do all the steps effortlessly, taking care not to put stress on the body. With practice the body will become more flexible.
- Avoid distractions such as chatting with others or talking on the phone in the middle of the exercise.
- Do not stop mid-way; complete all the steps.
- If you get very tired after doing *Suryanamaskar*, do *Shavasan* or *Yognidra*, but try not to fall asleep!
- Do not perform the exercise very late at night.

Caution

Menstruating women should not do *Suryanamaskar*. Those suffering from heart ailments, high blood pressure or any other serious ailment should do *Suryanamaskar* only after consulting a yoga expert or doctor.

This exercise method is a group activity and proves more beneficial if done in a group. When the mantras associated with *Suryanamaskar* are chanted collectively, the resulting vibrations are good for the body.

Now, we will learn about the various steps involved in doing *Suryanamaskar*.

The first step is to stop all thoughts going on in the mind, and try to focus on what we are doing. Since we are worshipping the Sun God while doing *Suryanamaskar*, we should say a prayer such as:

'Guide me in doing *Suryanamaskar*. Destroy all the illnesses in my body and while I worship you, please help my mind to concentrate.'

Now, close your eyes, breathe in and start reciting the first of the 13 Surya Mantras.

ESTABLISHED STATE: TADASAN / NAMASKARASAN / NAMAN MUDRA

Of the five physical organs of the body, it is extremely important that our hands and legs (limbs of locomotion) are in perfect condition; however, we only seem to realize their importance when they start to pain.

It may be somewhat difficult to believe that more muscle action can be obtained in the abdominal wall or cavity by just standing easily and apparently immobile than by executing gymnastic movements. *Tadasana* has a curative as well as therapeutic value.

Join the heels and toes as shown in the illustration. Keep the body straight and erect. Join the palms of both hands and keep them in the *Namaskar Mudra*, with the thumb touching the chest. Inhale and exhale naturally; or let it be slightly long and deep. Let the chest jut out a little so that respiration can be a little long; this will increase the concentration of the mind. Ensure that the weight of the entire body is divided equally on both legs. This is the best way to do *Tadasana*, which in the yogic syllabus, is the first *asana* or posture.

In this position, there is complete mobility of the chest, hence, respiration is performed very consciously, cautiously, perfectly, and evenly or uniformly. This is the best gift of *Tadasana*.

The human being, being the only animal that stands upright, must reckon with gravity which is always tending to pull organs downwards. He can counteract this ability with the help of *Suryanamaskar* and maintain correct posture while standing in *Tadasana*.

STEP 1: UDHARVA NAMASKAARASAN

Follow the picture and release both hands from the previous *mudra*; take them behind in the same line as the shoulder, giving a curve to the back. While doing this, slowly breathe in.

Each one of us, be it a child or an elderly person, has aches and pains in the neck, back, shoulder, waist or joints sometime or the other. A pain in the neck area not only is a hindrance while doing work, it also shows its impact in other regions like the back, head, hands, shoulders, fingers, eyes, nape of the neck and chest.

In order to give rest to the neck, and to stretch the spinal cord from within, one needs to bend the neck behind. This exercise when done regularly makes the neck relaxed and through practice, the pain will come under control and the muscles will become firm. In all steps of *Suryanamaskar*, one should do the movements of the neck, spinal cord, and hands very carefully, laying only the appropriate amount of stress and making the movements gracefully.

People of middle age can improve the mobility of their chests in this position to a remarkable degree by correcting their breathing at this stage; by increasing mobility they are helping to delay the advent of senile rigidity.

STEP 2: HASTAPADASAN / PADHASTASAN

Bend forward and touch your toes. Place the palms next to the feet and touch your forehead to the knees; the chin should touch the chest in this position. Breathe out. If you

wish to hold this position for a few seconds, then continue doing deep abdominal breathing - lift your stomach slightly as you breathe out and vice versa as you breathe in.

What more beauty can we expect from *Suryanamaskar* than the fact that the *asanas* can be done easily and effortlessly? If a plant is not looked after when it is young, it dies or like a neglected wild plant becomes stunted, shrinks or does not flourish. Same is the case of our muscles; if we do not do any exercise or *asanas*, they too shrink, all the veins in our body become constricted and joints become stiff. Due to limited movements, the spine muscles become stiff and hard too. When one reaches this stage where it becomes difficult to move, we rush to the doctor but by then it is very late!

In short, we misuse our body organs, or over use them, neglect them completely or sometimes don't use them at all. There are other reasons why one can get backaches, mental disorders, anemia, tension, depression, hysteria, over stress, worries, fear of depression, obesity, etc.

This step is very unique and has the following benefits:

- Helps to reduce abdominal and back pain (lumbago) during menstruation.
- Relieves physical and mental exhaustion.
- Relieves stomachache to some extent.
- Slows down heartbeats.
- Tones the kidneys, liver and spleen.

Caution

- Be very careful if you have a spinal disc disorder or slipped disc. Ensure that your back or spine remains concave throughout.
- Those who are prone to acidity, indigestion or dizziness should practice this step with the legs apart.
- Beginners: lift your toes and press your heels downwards towards the floor as you bend forward. Instead of your palms, you can rest your fingertips on the floor, until you get more flexible. Also, stretch your torso forward and press the front of your soles down on the floor. Extend your thighs from the knees to the hips.

STEP 3: DAKSHINAPAD PRASARNASAN

In this step, take the left foot behind with the toes touching the ground. The right knee should be bent, hands straight, elbows straight; rest the tips of the fingers on the ground.

Refer to the picture. While taking the leg behind, breathe in and hold it if possible. In this state, the back is stretched.

This stretch should be smooth and natural. Do not stress the spine too much. If we do this *asana* regularly, we can avoid hip and backache. Nature has one rule: muscles and joints which are used regularly will always get blood circulation and nourishment whereas those muscles and joints which are not exercised will get less nourishment and experience pain! *Suryanamaskar* has the capability of bringing about a certain amount of firmness in the joints and muscles, and strengthens the muscles and skeletal system.

Benefits of this step:
- Enhances lung capacity if you inhale up to the brim.
- Tones the muscles of the heart and chest.
- Gives relief from sciatic and arthritic pain.
- Improves digestion and helps to eliminate waste products by facilitating peristaltic and segmenting movements of the intestines.
- Reduces fat from the waist and the hips.
- Maintains steadiness.
- Stretches both sides of the body equally and intensely from top to toe.

Take care to come out of the step gradually. You will find that the mind has become tranquil and passive.

STEP 4: DWIPAD PRASARNASAN

In this state, take the right leg near the left leg. Now rest the palms and toes on the ground. In this state, the hip should be above the ground. Now touch the chin to the chest. The toes, hip and hands should form a triangle. When you lift up the hips, breathe out.

The bones of our body are like the trunk of a tree. A tree trunk has branches, fruits, flowers and creepers. Similarly, the structure of our body, which means our hands, legs, and veins, rests on our skeletal system. A creeper has the support of the tree; similarly, the veins have support of the bones. It is important that the trunk of the tree should be

strong; likewise, our bones, joints and muscles have to be strong. This step is very useful to gain strength.

STEP 5: SASHTAANK PRANIPAATASAN / CHATURANG DANDASAN

In this step, one should touch the forehead, chest, both the palms, both knees, and the toes on the ground. Lift the hips up. The elbows should be up and stretched. When the weight of the entire body rests on the hands, the shoulders will feel stressed. This is the position we are in when we prostrate ourselves in front of the gods, our elders and in the temple. This is an easy step but very effective.

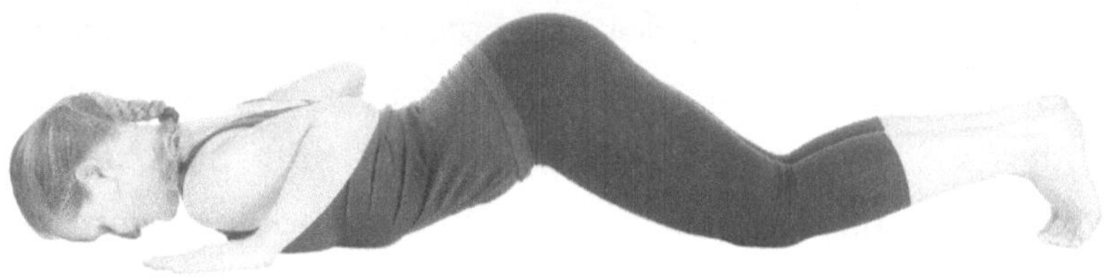

STEP 6: BHUJANGASAN / UDHARVAMUKH SHAVASAN

In this step known as the cobra pose, the knees and thighs should touch the floor. The hands should be straight, palms touching the ground, and elbows straightened; the body above the waist should be lifted up. Breathe in while lifting the body. Bend the head backwards and look up. Rest the toes on the floor and stretch the waist fully in the direction of the hands. The back should look like a bow.

This *asana* helps to keep the neck and spine flexible. This not only helps prevent spondylitis, but is also very advantageous for those who suffer from spondylitis. This step is very effective for the trunk and torso, which become stiff due to too much of tension, resulting in ailments like spondylitis and a very stiff back called ankiolosis. This step helps the neck and shoulder muscles ease out and the flexibility of the neck increases, easing the tension that has accumulated for so long! This step is very helpful for those who sit for long hours working on the computer or those who have jobs with little physical activity.

The benefits are many:
- Enhances resistance to infections in a great way, stimulating the nervous system.
- Gives great relief from the symptoms of menopause as well as menstrual cramps and pains.
- Stimulates the pituitary, adrenal, pineal and thyroid glands.
- Improves blood circulation to the ovaries and tones them at the same time.
- Increases lung capacity and helps to maintain the elasticity of lung tissues; be careful however as the tissues are very delicate and fragile.
- Helps correct a prolapsed uterus by stretching the pelvic and pubic region.
- Tones the liver, spleen and both the kidneys.
- Prevents varicose veins as this step tones the legs, hamstring muscles as well as the ankles.
- Gives tremendous relief from lower backache and arthritic pain in the back as it tones the spine.
- Relieves depression, mood swings or anxiety during menopause; boosts your self-esteem and confidence.
- Energizes the heart and the lungs.

STEP 7: BHUDHARASAN / ADHOMUKH SHVAANASAN

In this step you have to lift your hips keeping the elbows and knees straight, head stretched in the direction of the knees, and chin touching the chest. The toes, hips, and hands should form a triangle. Breathe out in this step.

Beginners: inhale and then exhale fully, and then bend from your waist. One can bend both the knees and then place both the palms on the floor next to the feet.

This is a very good downward step. A severe headache and pain in the eyes can be warded off by giving the forehead support from the floor and bending the back properly. This step is also helpful to get rid of pain in the neck region. If there is stiffness in the joints of the hand you may experience severe pain while doing this movement.

This step has many benefits:
- Helps to prevent hot flashes during menopause.
- It keeps a check on heavy menstrual flow.
- Relieves pain in the heels and softens calcaneal spur
- Reduces stiffness in the shoulder blades and arthritis in the shoulder joints.
- Strengthens ankles and tones the legs.
- Helps slow down heartbeats and reduce pulse rate
- Calms the mind and gently stimulates the nerves to rejuvenate the whole body.
- Reduces stiffness in the heels and makes the legs strong and agile.
- Restores energy.

STEP 8: DAKSHINPAAD SANKOCHANASAN

Bring the left leg forward and bring the sole of the foot in between the palms as in the earlier position. Rest the right sole and knee on the ground and look up. When you reach this step, breathe in. In the third and the eighth step, changing the position of the legs and making them go forward and backward exercises both the legs simultaneously.

The leg that we take behind proves to be a foundation for the spine. This way, the muscles of the back are like a thread stretched well. Besides this, with every long breath, the contraction and expansion that takes place stretches the external and internal muscles of the body. *Pranayama*

(breathing techniques) is very beneficial because in a very calm state, all the muscles and cells get managed well. Their capacity also increases and they are not exhausted or fatigued. All the organs are active and function effectively.

STEP 9: HASTAPAADASAN / PADAHASTASANA

This state is a repetition of the second step. In this step, one should bring the right leg forward near the left leg. Rest both palms next to both the legs. The forehead should touch the knees and the chin should touch the chest. Straighten both the hands and legs. In this state, breathe out. Initially, touch the forehead on the knees and place the palms straight on the floor. When you keep the knees straight, there is a lot of stretch and that's why this state seems difficult; but regularity brings about flexibility and later this state becomes very easy to do.

Due to the bend in the back, there is not just external body movement but one can also feel it internally. Thus blood circulation also improves. The digestive system, circulatory system and respiration also become highly effective. The best effect is on our excretory system. Important organs like the kidneys and intestines definitely start to function efficiently.

STEP 10: TADASAN / NAMASKARASAN

This step is a repetition of the first step. The whole body should be straight; stand erect, joining both soles and toes. Your eyes should be in the same line as the tip of your nose. Both the palms should be joined together, thumbs touching the chest. In this state, you should fill your chest with fresh air. This state completes one *Suryanamaskar*. The next step begins a new cycle. Recite the next *Surya Mantra* and continue with the next few *Suryanamaskars*, as your body allows and breathing permits.

When we take a deep breath while looking at the rising sun, from that one breath, several minute energy particles enter our body and drench every cell with unlimited power. This helps our body to function and gives us strength.

There are four main components of all the steps of *Suryanamaskar*:
- Blood circulation and an excellent capacity for breathing or respiration.
- Flexibility of joints and muscles.
- Strength, stamina and endurance.
- Tenacity.

Tenacity means the capacity to work with consistency without getting exhausted. Each of these four components is independent of each other. Of these, if one is in place, it is not necessary that all others will also fall in place. Only if all these components prosper well, will the body capacity increase and one will benefit from all the 10 steps of *Suryanamaskar*.

TWELVE

MAKE SURYANAMASKAR PART OF YOUR LIFE

Good health is a choice we all must make. The past has an immense impact on us, on our entire character. Often, past habits and our upbringing pull us back. Sometimes, self control alone is not enough to change habits like laziness or emotions like greed and jealousy, which have embedded themselves in our system. One needs a scientifically perfect program in place and the help of a person whom one can trust.

Let us take a situation we all can relate to - getting out of a warm, cozy bed early in the morning. We have a choice, either to continue to laze in the warm bed or step out and enjoy the early morning bliss. Getting out of bed is a small action but it has a large impact! It is a victory over our own self. This feeling stays with us through the day and boosts our self-confidence to face new challenges. From such small acts, one is able to win bigger issues in life. *Suryanamaskar* is extremely beneficial in bringing about discipline.

The entire cycle of *Suryanamakar* energizes, trains, and educates the neuro-muscular and neuro-glandular systems. Practicing it daily ensures adequate supply of fresh oxygenated blood. It brings perfect harmony to all the systems and organs of the body, thus invigorating the entire psychosomatic system of the human constitution.

Suryanamaskar is highly effective in eradicating ailments like blood pressure, diabetes, asthma, headache, depression, skin disorders, eye problems and other complications related to the mind. The infra-red rays coming from the sun and the heat that it produces prove beneficial in the treatment of neuralgia, neuritis, arthritis and sinusitis.

We know that in any kind of pain, heat plays an important role. Heat gives the body appropriate natural oils and brings them to the surface thereby, protecting it and making it soft. Strong sun rays kill germs in the air, water, fungi, virus, yeast molds and mites. The ultra-violet rays kill the germs on our skin. The rays of the sun are useful treatment for skin related skin disorders like diaper rash, athlete foot, psoriasis, impetigo and acne. When the body is exposed to the rays of the sun at a particular time and in a moderate way, they certainly save the skin from the harmful effects of the ultra violet rays and provide natural protection.

The effects of *Suryanamaskar* are far more effective than going to a gym and each one of us needs to personally examine this on our own. Everyone benefits from this exercise, be it a laborer doing hard work in the sun or one doing a desk job, a student or a truck driver on the move. *Suryanamaskar* has the potential to be the best method of exercise across the globe.

The tremendous power of *Suryanamaskar* cannot be understood unless it is experienced firsthand. *Pranayama*, which is part of *Suryanamaskar*, also helps in controlling elevated sugar levels, blood pressure and weight.

Exercises which increase flexibility like brisk walking, running, swimming, cycling, skipping, aerobic exercises and dance are helpful while doing *yogasanas*, as it helps in effective respiration. Yoga steers one to a contented, satisfied life. When we are calm it has a positive effect on our health & when we embark on this journey of exercise, we are sure to enjoy life and find the essence of life.

Our ancient Masters/*Acharyas* say that things in the external world cannot be changed by anyone, then why not look within our own selves and bring a metamorphosis of self? Yoga helps you to focus on the self and bring about a change. It is like an elixir for all ailments and an easy, effortless way to stay healthy and happy.

Suryanamaskar will change your life. Make a pledge to incorporate it into your daily routine today!

Great Reasons to Integrate Suryanamaskar into Your Daily Routine
1. Raises your self-image and self-esteem.
2. Wards off arthritis and other issues of joints.
3. Strengthens your bones.
4. Boosts your brain and memory power.
5. Relieves stress, tension and anxiety.
6. Wards off metabolic disorders, heart disease, diabetes and high blood pressure.
7. Lowers the risk of cancer.
8. Increases your libido.
9. Improves mood and cognition.
10. Beats clinical depression.
11. Maintains good body shape.

APPENDIX I

SURYANAMASKAR Vs. OTHER FORMS OF EXERCISE

How does *Suryanamaskar* score over other forms of exercise? The following are some of the defects of other systems of physical training or exercises:

- The time to be invested per day is usually too much.
- The routines involve a large number of movements, many of which affect only the arms and legs.
- Exercises affecting the internal abdominal organs are always done with the abdominal walls rigid; this has the effect of squeezing and fixing the internal organs, thus preventing the free action of the involuntary muscles of the intestines.
- Just a few minutes of exercise per day is not sufficient to counteract the wrong posture or wrong postural habits that are being habitually adopted.
- The stiff military position is adopted practically in all standing movements.
- The muscles of the waistline are largely neglected, or not taken into account, while those of the limbs are subjected to relatively excessive action.

- In breathing techniques, instead of standing with ribs mobile and puffing out the chest as the lungs are filled, the chest is first forced forward and the lungs are filled. It could lead to rigidity of the chest region (a spirometer reading will convince that the vital capacity is less when this procedure is adopted than in the former case).
- Often the cultivation of muscle for the mere sake of muscle is the be-all and end-all of training.

APPENDIX II

FAQs

When should I practice *Suryanamaskar?*
You can practice it at any time. Ideally, it should be done at sun rise or sun set.

Can I practice after eating food?
Ideally, you should practice on an empty stomach and after the bowels have been emptied in the morning. Ensure that there is a gap of four hours after a meal before you start the practice.

Should I do *Pranayama* and then *Suryanamaskar* or the other way around?
If you are a beginner in yoga practice, then DON'T do Pranayama. Just focus on your physical exercises. The breathing patterns in *Suryanamaskar* amount to *Pranayama* + yoga combined!

I have a pain in my back when I do *Suryanamaskar;* should I stop?
No. If required you can avoid the particular pose that causes you pain and continue with the rest of the poses. However, if the pain gets worse every time you practice, stop and consult a doctor.

When should I have a bath, before or after doing *Suryanamaskar*?

It is your convenience that matters. I find I am more flexible when I do *Suryanamaskar* after a bath. If you perspire a lot during the exercise regime, a bath is certainly recommended after practice.

How much time should I wait to eat after doing *Suryanamaskar*?

You can eat after 15 to 20 minutes.

Can I combine *Suryanamaskar* with jogging, swimming, or other workouts?

I recommend doing any outdoor exercise for three days a week, and *Suryanamaskar* for three days a week. Or, if possible, 20 *Suryanamaskars* everyday followed by other routine exercises or as suggested by health and fitness experts.

Should I warm up before doing *Suryanamaskar*?

Absolutely not! *Suryanamaskar* itself is an excellent warm up exercise.

Should I do *Shavaasan* after *Suryanamaskar*?

Yes, it will help give you an excellent resting pulse rate. It is also a powerful tool to cool down the mind and body and sense complex or organs of perception.

How many *Suryanamaskars* should one do to get some results initially?
I recommend one start with five numbers initially.

Can I do *Suryanamaskar* without guidance from a teacher?
It may prove dangerous if you are suffering from any ailment or disease or any genetic or hereditary issue. I recommend you learn from a qualified yoga therapist or teacher.

My nostrils are blocked. I am not able to breathe in or breathe out properly. Can I do *Suryanamaskar*?
Yes, you can, but with care. Do not do deep breathing or *Pranayama*.

How many *Suryanamaskars* should I do?
It all depends on your stamina, endurance, lifestyle, working conditions, body weight, living conditions or environment.

Should I do it fast or slow?
I recommend you do it slowly. Even if you are a regular practitioner, the benefits of doing slow *Suryanamaskar* are higher in my view. After about a month of doing slow *Suryanamaskars*, gradually increase speed.

Should ladies do *Suryanamaskar* during menstruation?
Not at all.

Should one practice *Suryanamaskar* after an abdominal operation?
If you have recently undergone an abdominal surgery, like hernia, start with simple walking and avoid anything in the nature of free striding. Consult your surgeon before you start *Suryanamaskar*.

Should one practice *Suryanamaskar* after pregnancy?
After pregnancy we see a state of muscle flabbiness, especially in the stretched abdominal muscles. After consulting your attending gynecologist, start with suitable light exercise such as walking; do not directly jump to *Suryanamaskar*.

Dr. Nitin Unkule
Kaivalya Yoga Institute,
1013/16, Swastik Society,
Shivajinagar, Model Colony,
Pune 411 016.
Tel. : +9120-25653448, 25671167
Website:
www.kaivalyayogainstitute.com
www.maturedhealth.com

- Managing Committee Member, Symbiosis Society.

- Practicing Yoga for the past 38 years and has traveled abroad extensively to promote Yoga and Vedanta.

- Represented India as a Cultural Ambassador to France in 1984.

- His CD on Yoga has got the 'Best CD Award' in Australia.

- Conducted 'Reversal of Heart Disease Program' since 1997 for heart patients with Dr. Jagdish Hiremath at Poona Hospital & Research Center and until now rehabilitation done for over 15,000 heart patients and hundreds of cardiac patients have successfully bypassed their Bypass surgery.

- Also working with Dr. Shailesh Puntambekar at Galaxy Cancer Care Unit on Cancer Care with Yoga & Pranayam techniques.

- Ex-Chairman Health Care Committee, Mahratta Chamber of Commerce Industries & Agriculture, Pune.

- Written 15 books on Yoga in Marathi and English till date.

- Regularly contributing on health issues in local Marathi and English newspapers and various magazines.

- At present also engaged in research in music, yoga and its impact on various diseases and mental disorders with Heidelberg University in Germany.

- Playing Mandolin since 4 years to connect various Ragaas and ancient Indian Mantras.

- Received 'Professional Excellence Award' in 2005 from Rotary International Foundation, USA, as they were celebrating 100 years of services.

- 'Excellence in IT Award' by Suryadatta Educational Institute in 2014.

- At Global Forum for Health Research, Forum 5, Conference held at Geneva, Switzerland, in Oct. 2001, called by WHO, on Heart Disease and Neurological disorders.

- At Global Forum for Health Research, Forum 5, Conference held at Mexico, USA, in Nov. 2004, called by WHO, on Heart Disease.